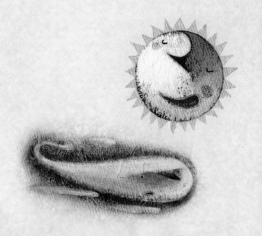

The Sun and the Wind

Based on a story by Aesop

Retold by Mairi Mackinnon

Illustrated by
Francesca di Chiara

Reading Consultant: Alison Kelly
Roehampton University

"Look at me," said the sun.

2

3

"Listen to me,"
said the wind.

4

"I'm strong,"
said the sun.

"I'm stronger,"
said the wind.

8

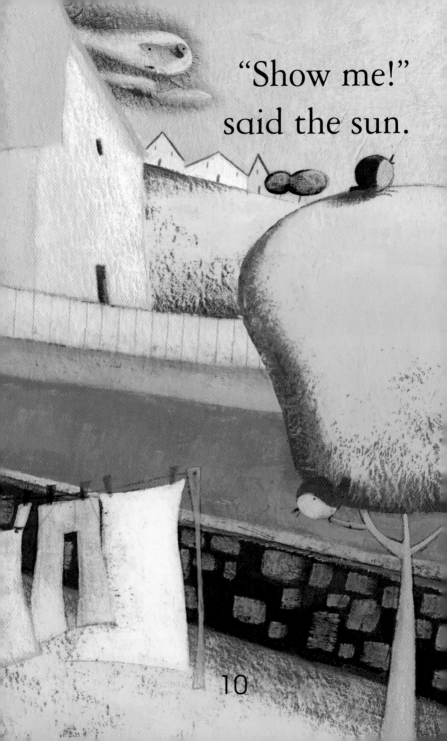

"Show me!"
said the sun.

10

"See that man?
Can you take
his coat off?"

"All right,"
said the wind.

15

"He's hiding!
My turn," said the sun.

16

19

20

"I win," said
the sun.

"Huff!" said the wind.

PUZZLES
Puzzle 1
Can you see..?

a ball   a sandcastle   a dog

a cake   a bird   a blanket

Puzzle 2
What is the man doing?
Match the words to
the pictures.

B

A

eating   walking

C

D

hiding

running

Puzzle 3

Can you spot the differences between the two pictures? There are 6 to find.

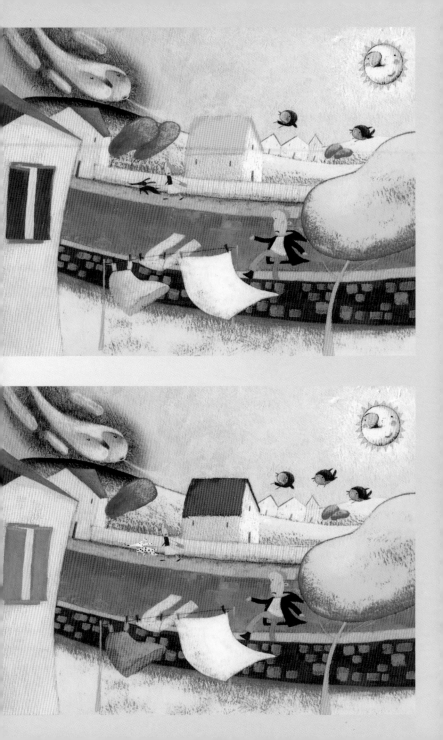

Answers to puzzles

Puzzle 1

a dog

a blanket

a bird

a cake

a ball

a sandcastle

Puzzle 2

A

B

C

D

running

hiding

walking

eating

 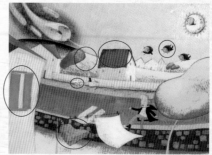

About the story

The Sun and the Wind is one of Aesop's Fables, a collection of stories first told in Ancient Greece around 4,000 years ago. Each story has a "moral" (a message or lesson) at the end.

31

Designed by Abigail Brown

Series editor: Lesley Sims

First published in 2007 by Usborne Publishing Ltd., Usborne House,
83-85 Saffron Hill, London EC1N 8RT, England. www.usborne.com
Copyright © 2007 Usborne Publishing Ltd.

32